What Love Is

A Fable for Our Times

Carol Lynn Pearson

Illustrated by
Kathleen Peterson

Salt Lake City

For Helen and LaVar,
who have shown us what love is.

C.L.P.
K.P.

First edition
03 02 01 00 99   5 4 3 2

Published by
Gibbs Smith Publisher
P.O. Box 667
Layton, Utah 84041
Orders: (800) 748-5439

Design by Randall Smith Associates
Edited by Suzanne Taylor
Printed and bound in Hong Kong

Library of Congress Cataloguing-in-Publication Data
Pearson, Carol Lynn.
    What love is: a fable for our times / Carol Lynn
Pearson; illustrated by Kathleen Peterson.
        p.   cm.
    ISBN 0-87905-918-4
    1. Married people — Poetry. 2. Love — Poetry.
    I. Peterson, Kathleen B., 1951–   II. Title.
PS3566.E227W47   1999
811'.54 — dc21   99-12670
                                            CIP

Their first touch
was at seventeen
when the moon was high
and her hair was soft
and her skin was warm
and her lips were full
and her heart beat fast
against his chest.

As he looked at her looking at him
he had never seen anything
so beautiful—

And he thought,

"Now I know what love is."

Another touch
was at twenty-three
when the rings were placed,
and the sun was high
and the church was bright
and her gown was lace.

As she looked at him
looking at her,
his eyes were moist
and his voice was soft
as he promised to be true forever—

And she thought,

"Now I know what love is."

Another touch
was at twenty-four
when they shook hands
on the deal they'd struck
that he would stop saying
when he saw her sneak a cookie,
"A moment on the lips,
Forever on the hips."
And she would stop
cutting out Ann Landers' column
whenever it talked about
what women want of men
and just *tell* him what she *needed*,
for crying out loud.

As she said, "I'm sorry,"
and he said, "Forgive me,"
they held each other tight
and laughed—

And they thought,

"Now I know what love is."

And he thought,

"Now I know what love is."

Another touch
was at twenty-eight
when he held her legs from shaking
and pressed her back
against the pain
while her body wrenched
and the head appeared.

As he held his son
he looked at her
and her hair was wild
and her skin was damp
and her eyes were closed
and he had never seen
anything so beautiful—

Another touch
was at thirty-four
when she kissed the back of his neck
and watched him disappear down the hall,
one arm holding the child
who had been sick all day
and the other arm holding the child
who had drawn flowers with Magic Marker
all over the new kitchen wallpaper
after having flushed her earrings
'bye-'bye.

As she sat in the recliner
and listened to him sing,
"Home, home on the range —
hey, hush, pardner,
the little lady needs quiet,"
she smiled —

And she thought,

"Now I know what love is."

Another touch
was at forty-two
when they gave high fives
on that jubilant day when
their boy graduated with a 3.8
and got the art department's first prize
and their daughter sang a small solo
in the school play
and was wearing the costume
she'd made all by herself
and landed a summer job
at Pizza Palace
and told them she didn't want
to pierce her navel after all.

"What a father these kids
must have!" she said.
"Ah, no," he said,
"you should see their mother!"

They hugged —

And they thought,

"Now I know what love is."

Thousands of touches
through the following years
in celebration
and in grief—

when she stroked his hair
and told him she just knew
he'd get another job soon,
and cheese sandwiches are her favorite—

when the sunset from the front porch
was too lovely to watch alone

when they got that call
from the officer
in the middle of the night
about their son

when she got "employee of the year"
after the kids were launched
and he e-mailed everyone he knew

when they strolled the beach on Maui
after twelve years of putting
all their quarters in a row of jars

when their daughter moved back in
during her divorce

when they shared the first tomato
their first grandchild
grew all by herself

when all the children and grandchildren
were with them at Thanksgiving
and each one had a long list
of gratitudes.

Their final touch
was at eighty-nine,
and her heartbeat rose
on the monitor beside her bed
as it always did
when she heard his walker in the hall.

Her hair was thin
and her skin was cold
and her lips were dry,
but she blew him just a hint of a kiss,
which he caught with a hand that shook
and pressed it to his cheek
where the tear was.

As he looked at her looking at him
silent and smiling,
he had never seen anything
so beautiful—

And they knew that they knew
what love is.